THE SIX VOYAGES OF
PLEASANT
FIELDMOUSE

TOR BOOKS BY JAN WAHL

The Furious Flycycle
The Six Voyages of Pleasant Fieldmouse
The S.O.S. Bobomobile*

(*forthcoming)

THE SIX VOYAGES OF
PLEASANT
FIELDMOUSE

JAN WAHL

TOR

A Tom Doherty Associates, Inc. Book

Cover and interior art by Tim Bowers

A Tor Book
Published by Tom Doherty Associates, Inc.
175 Fifth Avenue
New York, N.Y. 10010

Tor® is a registered trademark of Tom Doherty Associates, Inc.

ISBN: 0-812-52403-9

First Tor edition: July 1994

Printed in the United States of America

0 9 8 7 6 5 4 3 2 1

To My Two Voyagers, Marty and Ken

CONTENTS

FIRST VOYAGE
The Island
1

SECOND VOYAGE
The Big Pike
13

THIRD VOYAGE
The Lighthouse
24

FOURTH VOYAGE
The Muskrat and The Heron
35

FIFTH VOYAGE
The Plum Castle
54

SIXTH VOYAGE
The Tea-Strainer
69

FIRST
VOYAGE
~
THE ISLAND

On a warm, clear summer's day with the sun floating bright as butter, with caterpillars crawling along the grass, Pleasant Fieldmouse was busy, pounding narrow planks together until they fitted, one by one, making a kind of raft.

Then he added a rudder, with a firm steering handle, plus a mast for a topsail.

"Hello, Victoria," he said. He knew each green-and-pink caterpillar by name. Victoria nodded both ends of her. It was hard to tell if she was moving straight ahead or backing up.

"Are you anticipating a flood?" asked

1

Mrs. Worry-Wind Hedgehog, the champion forest worrier, emerging out of the wild strawberries. She was wringing her paws and tugging at her apron. She glanced at the raft very suspiciously.

"No," replied the fieldmouse, tapping the raft to make sure it was soundly constructed, "but I think it is time for me to go out in the world—and see what is happening." He believed that everybody, sometime, ought to be going someplace.

The best way to go was sailing, because then you could sit and think while you were going.

"What is out there that we don't have *here*?" wondered Mrs. Hedgehog, her eyes big now as plover's eggs. "Is it something WORSE?"

Pleasant looked at her calmly, adjusting the green-and-white bottle cap that said *Bubble Up*. He tied it on with thread. This became an impressive yachting hat.

He then peered out through the grasses,

where the gurgling stream met the vast, mysterious lake. "That is something I must find out for myself. I know the forest, however, by heart."

Mrs. Hedgehog tried her best not to worry over his decision. It was not easy, because worrying came naturally to her, as naturally as birds learn how to fly home after winter. Not worrying was difficult for that lady. Like holding your breath for ten minutes.

By pulling herself together, concentrating on the crystal sap of a wild cherry tree, she managed to make her eyes small as acorns, their own ordinary size.

"What will you name your boat?" she inquired, calm as Christmas for the moment.

Pleasant pondered that problem, scratching his long foot in the loose ground by the shore, trying out names. Tomato Surprise. Gorgonzola. Mermaid. "What about Fluffy?"

"Is that a name for a boat?" worried the cautious hedgehog.

"It is now," said Pleasant, who then got

out paint and paintbrush and drew in the name painstakingly, with anchors at each end of it.

FLUFFY

"It is a non-sinkable name," he declared quite hopefully.

Mrs. Hedgehog pulled off her apron, a cranberry-colored one. "Here, use this as your sail. And—may it return you to us unharmed!" Then she burst into loud tears, scrambling away, till the fieldmouse heard her sobs and hiccups dwindle into the distance.

"I must christen this ship," he announced to himself, then tapped the planks, thunk, with a long dried pod.

Thistles, soft and silky, flew out of the split pod, fluttering into the bright, cheerful air.

"I name you the *Fluffy*. And I dedicate to you my service!"

Then, he jumped aboard with tasty provisions, tied in tidy bundles, and pushed the *Fluffy* away from shore, silently leaving the forest. Nobody saw him depart.

Not even his friends, Haunted Beaver and

Never-Doubting Frog and Anxious Squirrel, who gathered in the late afternoon, searching under fern leaves and in his hammock and on the roof of the beaver's house, from where the fieldmouse liked to stand and gaze out to the far water. Finally they learned, from blubbering Mrs. Hedgehog, how and why he had gone. They were awed by the daring of his adventure.

"We had better start to dig the grave

now," worried Mrs. Hedgehog. "Those who go away seldom come back ALIVE."

For once they had to agree with her. Any animal who leaves to see what is happening is a strange animal. *They* wouldn't have left for anything.

The forest already seemed emptier, with Pleasant removed.

Graybeard Tortoise came shuffling forward, blinking, wondering what was up.

Some birds—chickadees and robins mostly —flew past the tree-crowns, and observed Pleasant to be just the tiniest speck disappearing out into the deep, mammoth lake. You could not see from one end of it to the other.

Not even the birds really could.

Pleasant stood proudly on his raft, letting his snaky tail drag behind in the cool water. He examined the wet blue lake all around, and the fading shoreline, and felt very thrilled. He also began to feel quite alone. Or was it the sharp chill of the evening, since the sun was falling down?

Pleasant looked at the sunset at the western end of the lake, very happy with it. How pleasant it was, as long as you had sunsets! In the forest, the tall trees, the high flowers, and the thick weeds usually hid the spectacle from him in the evening.

The sun went from pink to red-orange to purple, spreading its color: until nothing was

left but color shifting across the quickly-dimming sky.

Soon the stars came twinkling. There was a faint breeze moving the lake.

A small island loomed in front of him, thick and wild and grassy.

He steered over toward the green-purple island, deciding he could pitch camp there, in safety, for the night. There seemed to be nothing growing on it but scrubby trees and bushy reeds. It was the kind of place on which you could probably stay forever, if you didn't mind nobody to talk to.

However—the island was headquarters for a clan of green-and-gold ducks, who bolted forth, snapping viciously, to chase him away.

They had horrible, small, angry red eyes and quick, swishing wings like fans opening and shutting. They made a racket such as the fieldmouse had never heard in his life.

"All right, all right," crooned Pleasant to the ducks. "I respect your sanctuary. Whoa!"

Bravely he smiled, turning the rudder hard, to avoid the snap-snap from the ducks' bills.

The duck army crowded together, lined up in a row, daring him to TRY landing there.

"Not every island is what it seems," he said to himself thoughtfully.

So, in the nick of time, he drifted off, under the stars. . . . Then the sky behind the stars grew pitch-black; the moon lit the entire surface of the water.

The breeze stopped. The water's gentle lap-lapping stopped. The angry ducks quieted down. Soon he felt he was floating as if in a soundless dream; with the only noise his tail wiggling in the deep water.

SECOND
VOYAGE

THE BIG PIKE

Then Pleasant's tail got yanked, and in a jiffy he was pulled right off the raft, under the water.

He could not speak; his mouth was too full of water and bubbles. He was plummeting downward, being plunged far below the surface. Then his eyes became used to the glow of the underwater; he had to hold his breath.

The moonlight sank to the bottom of the lake. Some whitefish slipped by like liquid ghosts.

"Oh pardon me!" said a voice, and his tail

was released. The fieldmouse rose to the surface by kicking with his strong hind legs, and by lashing the water with his tail.

A swift big Pike swam alongside him.

"Please pardon me," repeated the Big Pike. "I thought your tail was something to eat."

"Well," said Pleasant, trying not to sink and trying to remain pleasant at all costs, "it is something to bite." He heard thousands of mayflies buzzing overhead. Nzzzzz. Nzzzzz.

The mayflies were dropping millions of eggs out of the sky, milky and sticky.

"I guess I'll join you after all," suggested Pleasant, and let the Big Pike pull him by the tail again (what else could he do?), swiftly beneath the water. The moonlit under-lake was shiny and transparent.

There, among the weeds, he saw snails and tadpoles shimmering; dimmer figures roamed in the distance. Carp and goldfish with flickering scales. Catfish. Water snakes. Bullheads and gizzard shad.

The Big Pike was about to help him make their acquaintance, showing him off.

"Wait. My two minutes are up. Can't—hold—my—breath—any—more," gulped Pleasant, kicking to the surface with his feet. The mayflies had flown on. The air was sweet and crisp.

Pleasant tried to shake the water out of his ears. "How do you get your breath all the time, underwater?" the interested fieldmouse asked the Big Pike, who had stayed close beside him.

"We breathe through our gills—we fish do," said the flat-nosed Big Pike, who had a low and throbbing voice. The Big Pike was pale in the moonlight. He hunted around, hungry for mayfly eggs. He found some floating and greedily gobbled them up.

"Oh, how would you like a quick trip around the lake?" suggested the Big Pike.

"I have a raft here. Somewhere," replied Pleasant, searching for it in vain; when you have built an excellent new raft, you hate to lose it so soon.

"I'm *faster*," boasted the Big Pike, who urged the fieldmouse to grab onto his back fin. The Big Pike lurched forward, cutting through the water. Pleasant heard a zinging in his ears.

Off they raced, with Pleasant scarcely having a chance to take a deep breath first.

Every time the Big Pike dived, Pleasant could feel it most in his whiskers. They rattled.

The Big Pike showed him beautiful glassy shells, and honeycombed rocks, and a sunken schooner—a two-masted vessel, gently rocking to nowhere, to and fro.

Since the Big Pike was the biggest fish around, the smaller fish did not bother him. Pleasant clung for dear life. "Hold on!" shouted the Big Pike wickedly, and Pleasant grew dizzy, whizzing behind.

"This is too fast for me!" Pleasant tried calling to the front end of the speeding fish. They dashed along as if swept in a great tornado.

"Are you getting dizzy?" asked the Big Pike, showing a glittering concern. He turned his head back to examine his little passenger. He had no teeth in his pale long head; but Pleasant, pretty vividly, remembered how he could bite.

The Big Pike surfaced, then dived, then surfaced, then dived—till his body shook, swallowing laughter.

Pleasant was beginning to put two and two together and absolutely was no longer able to enjoy the ride.

So he bit the Big Pike on his flank as sharply as he could with pointed rodent teeth. The Big Pike shuddered and groaned, then screamed, letting his rider go free.

"There must be a stingray loose in the lake!" bellowed the big fish, swimming for cover, forgetting his choice near-dinner. Pleas-

ant kicked his way to the surface (he was getting good at it), banging his head on a hard, solid object.

It was his raft, the *Fluffy* itself.

The fieldmouse climbed aboard and lay there, feeling like a cold, limp hot-water bottle. He suddenly sat up: his provisions were gone.

The night was vast.

A far, sad loon cried.

Pleasant was wet and hungry. His teeth chattered loudly. It took a long while for the moon to dry him. He ran around and around on the raft, in an effort to dry himself faster. Well, things were starting to happen.

He sat down, steering—and stared out over silvery waters. He heard a faraway growling.

It was his stomach, telling him something. It was telling him he was hungry. He knew how the Big Pike felt; when you are hungry, you listen to your stomach. He was happy to be aboard his own little raft. He tried to forget about food.

He tried to forget the provisions he'd

21

carefully packed. He tried to forget the still-warm mint-leaf cake. He tried concentrating on the great, round full moon. That brought him back to food again.

Pleasant Fieldmouse looked at the moon and the moon looked at him. He sniffed the clean night air.

He prayed:

> *Please give me now*
> *Another day,*
> *That I may find*
> *Some cheese.*
> *I ask it on my knees.*

And the raft carried him on.

THIRD
VOYAGE

~

THE LIGHTHOUSE

Cheerfully he greeted the morning. He had stayed awake the whole night, being watchful. He believed he might arrive at a desert, or at the foot of snowy mountains.

He followed a strong beam of light that shifted, moving in a wide arc, swinging slowly over the lake. He followed the beam until daybreak, when it was shut off.

It came from a tall, thick, white-painted tower that rose out of the lake on a small plot of ground, with only a neat row of hardy zinnias and bright hollyhocks circling it.

No mountains. No desert.

Pleasant had arrived at the Lighthouse, without knowing what a lighthouse was. He moored the raft, hopping ashore. He ran up toward the great white stucco tower and found a notice posted on the door.

GONE TO TOWN.

PLEASE WAIT.

SIGNED, GROVER BRIGGS.

A huge cat—speckled gray, with black-booted feet—was sunning itself on the door-step.

"I wonder, is there any cheese in there?" asked Pleasant, who didn't recognize a cat when he saw one, either. Not face-to-face. A cat was something he had vaguely heard about.

The Cat was sizing him up.

"No cheese. We're out of everything. Exactly what is it you're looking for?"

"Not a thing," said Pleasant. "Though I

might find something. I want to be where things are happening."

"Aren't they happening where you come from?" asked the Cat, gazing at him with growing curiosity.

"Yes—forest things, that's all. What is GROVER BRIGGS?" inquired the fieldmouse, looking at the sign on the Lighthouse door.

"That is my master," sighed the Cat, congratulating itself. This little fellow was strictly from the forest.

"What's a master?" wondered the fieldmouse, anxious to learn.

"A master is somebody who owns you," purred the lazy pet, astonished that he didn't know.

"How awful, to have somebody own you!" Pleasant reflected.

"No, I get milk everyday," said the Cat, licking its fur and waiting for the right moment to pounce.

"May I take a nap on the step beside you?" the fieldmouse asked, not realizing he was marching into new danger. "I would enjoy lying in the sun warming my bones."

"Tender bones," whistled the Cat quietly. "Certainly. Curl up beside me here. Two's company, they say."

"Who said that?" Pleasant wondered drowsily, snuggling closer to the thick fur, yet keeping out of the shady side. At first the concrete step was damp, however the warmth from his own body soon made the spot comfortable.

"Old fishwives said it," replied the Cat, no longer sleepy at all. "They sit there, being wise—while they clean the scales off caught fishes." The Cat got hungry thinking about *that*.

Yet it kept speaking in a drowsy, purring tone, so its little companion would not grow alarmed. "You haven't been out in the world much, have you?" it couldn't help demanding.

"Only since yesterday," admitted Pleasant Fieldmouse, sitting bolt upright. "You are clever to have guessed! I *admire* clever creatures like you!" He didn't want to show his ignorance or be impolite and ask what sort of animal this was; all he was sure of was that it had a nice, smooth, silky fur to snuggle against. "You are really clever!"

How then could the Cat consider making breakfast out of him? You can't eat an admirer.

"Not half so clever as you," grumbled the Cat, mostly to himself. It was angry with itself for missing out on breakfast. It hated the lake, and refused to fish for itself, ugh, sticking its paws in the water. The lighthouse-keeper, Mr. Briggs, had set out a pan of milk before he had left, but a horrible-looking leaf, that had been carried through the air for miles, or that, perhaps, had stuck to a bird's leg or wing, had drifted down into the pan.

Now the Cat had to be patient and wait for Mr. Briggs's return, when there would be Norwegian sardines.

The Cat was pretty particular. It often believed if it had lived on the mainland it would have taken prizes at cat shows. It preened itself, making doubly certain its cat-coat was silky and glistening.

Pleasant spied the kitty bowl.

Since he came from the forest (where anything was anybody's, depending on who got to it first), he arose and scurried over, removing the unsightly leaf, and started lapping up the milk.

"Listen—you have a few things to learn. That milk is MINE," warned the cat abruptly, leaping off the step. Pleasant stepped back, else he would have been knocked silly.

"You mean you are its master?" he inquired, watching the Cat survey the now-delicious-seeming milk.

"Take off your hat when you talk to me," hissed the furry Cat, getting milk on its whiskers. "Now, dip your hat in." Pleasant untied the thread and removed his hat. He dipped it in the milk, as he was told.

Then, he had his own tiny pan, which he put on the ground and drank from.

"Just two chums, aren't we?" muttered

the Cat, who couldn't believe what it had let happen. "Look, why don't you skedaddle *out* of here? While I'm still on best behavior?"

"Aren't you always AS YOU ARE NOW?" questioned the fieldmouse, trying to imagine its worst behavior, without succeeding. But he could only take creatures as they seemed to be. To tell the truth, he was a forest person and he knew best, there, who his genuine enemies were—Tired Fox and Terrible Owl. Out in the world, you had to learn the false from the true every minute. "I think it's nice for you to let me be master of your milk too," he added.

The Cat coughed and studied the purple, yellow, and red zinnias and papery hollyhocks. What could it *do* about him?

The sky was lemon-colored and a warm wind blew over the lake.

"Good-bye, then. I had better be getting off," Pleasant announced, reluctantly, and took command of his raft once more. The Cat sauntered up to the water's edge and briefly debated thanking him for removing the leaf from the milk bowl.

Pleasant was going to ask for directions from his new friend; next he decided, yes, what he would find he would find, so that seemed more satisfactory.

"Good-bye," called out the Lighthouse

Cat, and it would not forget him. It grumbled all the way, following him on its padded feet.

What had gotten into its head? Thinking of thanking him!

It watched him cast off—then rushed back to the step, where Pleasant's bottle-cap hat still lay, cuffing it meanly with its paw. "Take that, you dumb hat!" growled the Cat. "And that!"

But Pleasant was splendidly sunning himself on his raft, *Fluffy*; and what he didn't know didn't hurt him.

FOURTH
VOYAGE

THE MUSKRAT
AND THE HERON

The warm breezes stirred, rippling the lake, filling out the cranberry-red sail that was Mrs. Hedgehog's apron. Pleasant sighted across to the shore growing nearer, viewing the country sliding toward him.

He half-realized he had no hat any longer, without recalling where he'd left it. He was too excited by the prospect of finding Something New. His heart was beating like a tom-tom.

The fieldmouse fully believed he was arriving at the opposite shore of the large lake. Actually he was returning to the very same side he had started out from. But at the farthest tip, in the direction of the City.

There was a cattail marsh going off from the lake. Blue water was no longer under him—there lay squishy dark-brown mud and thick, slimy grasses, among which cattails sprouted.

The *Fluffy* all at once had got a mind of its own. He couldn't steer it anymore by using the rudder.

The weeds spread apart and the raft rushed on, leaving bubbles and bright circles on the surface behind it.

Soon he discovered, by peeking over the edge, there was somebody submerged below it. That is, his raft was being *carried* on someone's back.

That somebody turned out to be a silvery-brown muskrat, whose name was Solitude.

The muskrat was guiding him to his house, and wedged the raft securely, hiding it among the marsh grass.

"Wait a minute!" protested Pleasant. Sol-

itude simply waved with one paw in the direction of an ash tree at the edge of the marsh. An unfriendly looking heron was sitting, waiting, on a skinny gray branch.

"Can you swim?" Solitude asked Pleasant, then without pausing for an answer tugged him off the raft.

Down he went again!

Pleasant was tired from hours of steering and being watchful. All he knew was that he

trusted this fellow—not because of his man-
ners, which were rather coarse, but because of
the goodness which was shown in him, even
by his velvety hands, and feet, and tail.

Holding onto the muskrat was not like
holding onto the skin of the Big Pike; Solitude's
pelt was warm and friendly. Down they dived,
straight into the marsh water, and journeyed
through a long passageway, a secret tunnel it
was, and, at last, bobbed up in a small two-room
igloo made of densely packed cattails.

There was a bedroom and a dining room,
simple rooms, kind of pleasant. It was almost
pitch-dark in there, cozy and damp.

He was offered a meal of lilies and water
chestnuts. And the fieldmouse gratefully
munched them.

"Did you tell me your name was Grati-
tude?" Pleasant asked, when his mouth got
empty.

"No, Solitude," said Solitude, chewing.
"Means I like to be alone a lot."

"Well—I guess I must be the opposite,"

declared the fieldmouse, considering himself and how he was. "I miss my forest friends; however, they are stick-at-homes, and lack adventure in their souls!"

The muskrat looked hurt. "There's nothing wrong with being a stick-at-home," he insisted, wiping his shiny dripping nose. "The safest thing there is!"

Pleasant believed that a perfectly reasonable point of view. Although it was not very adventurous, not very poetic. Now the muskrat was contented with the wet and the dark, because he knew no better. The fieldmouse preferred it sunny; he was remembering meadows with clover blossoms, and open, clear skies above.

Still, the muskrat was poor but generous. So, as a guest, the fieldmouse didn't have much to complain about—except for the funny smell in the place.

"Don't you ever have an itch to roam?" questioned Pleasant.

"Itch? ITCH?" pondered the dull but

kindly Solitude. Obviously he didn't even understand. The fieldmouse tried another way: "I like surprises, now and then," he admitted. He happened to look at the lily roots.

Solitude wondered, "Would you like salt and pepper on your lilies?"

"Thank you, no," said Pleasant, surprised. "I don't think so; never had any." The salt and pepper had been dropped by duck-hunters the autumn before in little packets, next to the marsh, and Solitude had saved them for special occasions.

The fieldmouse's eyes were becoming heavier . . . and heavier; his arms ached from all the steering. There was a powerful smell, such as there is when muskmelons grow ripe.

"Maybe you would be kind enough to let me take a snooze?" he murmured.

And he fell asleep right at the table while holding a lily stalk.

The muskrat carried him easily into the tiny alcove, between the dining room and the

bedroom, and deposited the little figure on a pallet of dry rushes.

Then, Solitude himself, first checking to see that the front gate of twigs was secure, and that no one would burst in in the dark, threw himself onto his own bed, staring up at the black, black ceiling, delighted he had company for a change.

Pleasant awoke in the damp house finding

it was still dark, smelling the heavy scent again, hearing Solitude moving about, humming and sneezing.

Solitude offered him a cup of hot root-tea, taking one cup himself. Solitude sneezed and almost dropped the cup.

"It's nothing," the muskrat promised. "Only a very nasty late summer cold."

Nevertheless, the fieldmouse after breakfast decided his host ought to be back in bed, lying down.

Pleasant announced he was going to walk around a bit outside and pick some watercress. "What you need is Gramma Fieldmouse's watercress soup."

"Be careful, every step!" warned Solitude, having to cover up a sneeze that shook the entire igloo. "I was hoping to teach you how to slide down the mud-chute," fretted the muskrat. "Had the whole—*kerchoo*—day planned!"

Pleasant ducked out through the lengthy tunnel, emerging in the middle of marsh-

tangles. He was about to brush away some
sticky weeds, his mind on watercress, when he

was lifted straight up into the air, by the scruff of his jacket, by the spear-billed Heron.

He shuddered to find himself traveling through the air, the lake falling away under his feet. "HAAA! HAAA! HAAA!" screeched the great Heron, who flew with her neck bent in an S-shape.

The Heron deposited him high in a poplar tree, in a nest (on a platform) with two pale-blue eggs.

"Crush my babies and it's the end of *YOU!*" screamed her horrible shrieking voice. She instructed Pleasant to baby-sit with the eggs. And she gave him a gold watch-chain to look at, while she was off. *She* was big enough to swallow him, that he knew.

It was hard to view her in a kindly way, no matter how hard he concentrated on it. He tried for a few minutes, after she had flown away beyond the branches of the high tree; nevertheless, the most pleasant thing he could think of was to get out of there. Pronto.

He carried the gold watch-chain with him,

though it did slow up his progress. It kept catching on twigs and knobs . . . till there were no more branches, just the trunk below, with a long drop to the ground.

He would have to find another way to get down.

One of the branches above hung out over the edge of the lake; so he used the chain to hoist himself back up, instead. Inch by inch by inch.

The chain was quite heavy for him, and he nearly lost his balance several times.

At last he reached the branch, which jutted out like a stretched-out arm. He had to creep out to the very end of it, till the branch swayed crazily even from his miniature weight.

He threw the gold chain down to the water first. Then followed it with his own body.

Bloop!

He hit with terrific force.

For an instant he thought he had landed upon the ground by mistake, but he was not

broken—only wet. He scanned the blue sky, watching for the possible return of the errand-going Heron. He was learning how to be pleasant but cautious.

With a watery sneeze, Solitude came out of the water beside him, his brown fur dripping; he had fetched the sunken chain. Some mud-puppies bobbed up too for an instant, startled to find a mouse in their midst.

Pleasant and Solitude struggled out and crawled onto the marsh shore, where it was awfully muddy. Pleasant was wringing out his coat, which now was torn and dirty and shabby-looking. He himself was pretty bedraggled.

Solitude had followed him after his long absence from the cattail igloo, sensing danger. Muskrats cannot climb poplar trees, therefore Solitude had had to wait in the water, trying not to sneeze.

Now he sneezed and sneezed.

"Are you going to continue your journey?" Solitude inquired regretfully, between sneezes.

"No, I'm going to STAY and help nurse you," Pleasant decided. "We must collect that watercress for the soup." So they did, and hung it on the watch-chain, each carrying one end of the gold chain.

Gramma Fieldmouse's watercress soup

soon was boiling away and smelling savory. Pleasant bundled Solitude up in an eiderwort blanket and poured the soup down him. "But I *always* have a cold," said the muskrat; "it is part of my way of life! I live in the moist earth!"

"It is not too late to change," advised the fieldmouse.

After a number of days of this treatment, Pleasant pulled Solitude out-of-doors by moonlight and sat him upon a dry moss stool.

And he did a little dance, making circling motions with his paws.

"Pretty little moon, shine on me, shine on Muskrat too. Make Muskrat well! Shine on us! Listen to me!"

And it seemed Solitude might sneeze; but suddenly he didn't. "Guess it worked," Solitude said, amazed.

Then the fieldmouse hurried his patient back to bed again and wrapped him up and ladled out another dose of soup. By this time Solitude was so full of soup he began to groan.

The fieldmouse sat by the invalid's bed and the two of them talked by the hour. They got on very well together. They each explained their points of view.

Pleasant would declare it was fine to venture out in the world and look around.

Solitude would declare it was safer not to.

Pleasant was a busy nurse, bustling back and forth with hot nutritious soup. He was convinced the patient must be improving under this treatment.

So it happened one morning, from his bed, Solitude saw the fieldmouse brushing his torn jacket and smoothing out his whiskers and he was sure Pleasant wanted to move on. It wasn't difficult to guess that.

Pleasant went out to check the weather. The weather was in perfect shape.

Solitude wrapped himself in his blanket, for fear of making Pleasant unhappy, and followed him out. The muskrat inquired if it was true he would be leaving.

"You are 100 percent right," sighed

Pleasant. "I would like to take my raft up this creek, as soon as possible."

He pointed to the creek that emptied into the lake. He had had enough of the wetness and the dampness and the darkness.

So Solitude told him about an ancient lady, Old Aunt Raccoon, who might repair his torn jacket and allow him to wash and rest up. Old Aunt Raccoon lived along the creek, not too far distant, on the edge of a famous potato farm.

"Give her my name and she won't eat you," instructed Solitude. "She knows a cousin of mine."

He loaded Pleasant's raft up with good a supply of lilies and water chestnuts, and as Pleasant was casting off he called out:

"You'll smell apples in the orchards, then grapes. Then—her house is next! Give my regards to the world!"

Next he was gone, with a splash, shucking off the eiderwort blanket.

Following the stream, pushing his way with a pole against the current since he did not want to be swept headlong back into the lake, Pleasant struggled (it was hard work) out of the cattail country up the creek toward the orchard country and Old Aunt Raccoon's—keeping his sharp ears open for the angry whirring overhead of heron wings.

Instead, he thought he heard one loud, terrific, ear-shattering, exploding Sneeze.

FIFTH
VOYAGE

THE PLUM CASTLE

The flies and bluebottles zoomed in the air. Bullfrogs were croaking from the deep. Bees buzzed and shook down pollen dust. Sparrows chattered while they flew. Otters swam behind him, playing, churning up the wrinkled water. The stream was crowded, above and below.

On the banks on either side, end-of-summer flowers were out: goldenrod, asters, black-eyed Susans, butter-and-eggs—their yellow blazing with sunshine.

Wet snails moved their houses over slimy rocks. A snake with black and red rings

painted over him oozed down the clay bank and gazed at Pleasant Fieldmouse with terrible, tiny eyes.

He poled his raft quickly along, whistling to himself softly but cheerfully.

Was it the heat? He was thinking how it would be to be home swinging in his grass hammock.

When it was evening, with the katydids making a huge racket, he smelled the fruit orchards, then the grapes, then the potatoes, and he knew the place he saw must belong to Old Aunt Raccoon.

The shadows were growing long.

Pleasant knocked on the door and looked up and immediately gave the old lady Solitude's name. She repaired his jacket and let him take a bath. In return, he weeded her garden by moonlight.

When he was working, hoeing the spearmint, Old Aunt Raccoon came out and made a hole in the earth with a stick and then put her furry ear to the hole, listening.

Then, seemingly satisfied, she went back into the house and stood at the lighted doorway. Pleasant was tempted to put his ear to the hole, listening, also.

Yet *something* told him he should not, that she might rush out and gobble him up, so he kept working and weeding the garden. It was a mystery; still, every mystery need not be solved, he was beginning to believe.

When he was finished, Old Aunt Raccoon took him to some potato sacks, filled but not yet tied, in which he might snuggle, safely sleeping that night. Then, she shut and bolted her own door; for when you live amid the open landscape—no matter what animal you are—you are unprotected. He tried sleeping with one eye open. Soon that eye closed and he slept, dreaming of the forest, green and lovely, dreaming that everybody missed him very much; and that, when he returned, he would bring them each a fine potato, tied in a ribbon.

When the fieldmouse awoke he was in a truck, bouncing and jouncing along a bumpy road. He was in a scratchy sack that said, in red letters,

SELECTED POTATOES

58

He gnawed his way out of his cloth prison. The truck was heaped high with sacks of potatoes.

Through a crack in the side rails of the truck he saw it was still bitter black out. The truck roared down the road, and when it hit bumps, the potatoes shifted, rubbing against each other. It was much safer *out* of the sack.

The truck stopped; then suddenly wheeled backward, causing him to tumble head-over-tail. Men were talking together loudly. His heart jumped when the double doors, with a great sharp clang, were flung open. Pleasant scuttled back into the sack, which soon was being carried.

Footsteps (heavy shoes with cleats on) went back and forth; voices continued, then faded away. It was silent again except for the ticking of a clock. Pleasant knew it was not the sound of his heart: his heart was thumping, not bumping. Even through the burlap he began to smell the most beautiful smell he had ever smelled.

He may not have recognized a cat, but he recognized cheese. "My prayer was answered," he said, full of wonder. He crawled out to find himself in paradise.

He scrambled on top of a case of Mrs. Weiss's Sauerkraut with Caraway Seeds.

The morning light, just coming in, filled the whole place with a yellow-gray mist.

Here were kippers, codfish cakes, smoked oysters, and herring-with-mustard! Salami!

Pepperoni! Thüringer sausage! Danish bacon! Lapsang souchong and jasmine tea! Artichokes! Avocados! Eggplants! And okra! Meats and fish and vegetables galore. His whiskers prickled and he felt faint from the heady mixture of odors.

What manner of place can this be? he asked, but guessed, at once, he might be in the City.

He ran to the large front window on which was painted something he could not read:

DNA RECORGNEERG

NESSETACILED

because from where he stood it was backwards.

At last he could not stay away one minute longer from the exotic cheeses: Dutch Gouda! French Brie and Roquefort! Welsh Caerphilly! English Stilton! Italian Mozzarella! German Liederkranz! He shuffled across the waxed floor blissfully, slowly making up his mind which he would first select, when doors opened, lights flicked on, tall men streamed in and put on long blue-and-white aprons. The store was opening.

Pleasant rushed to the front, where some-one had built a castle of jars of Plums With Brandy.

He leaped through one of the window-spaces, having to stay there the whole day—so near, yet so far! Jars, in long rows, of pepper relish and corn relish, hid the cases of gorgeous cheese. However, the symphony of odors made him tremble constantly, and he wished there wasn't so much coming and going.

Out of curiosity he peeked, just once, out from the castle window. He looked straight in the eye at a lady who grew a gar-den on her hat.

The lady tottered, slightly. Then she turned to one of the solemn gentlemen wearing blue-and-white aprons.

"Did I see a mouse?" she asked.

The steady clock ticked.

The solemn gentleman was polishing a bottle of pears with a cloth—polish, polish. "Madam, we have never, *NEVER* had a mouse. I swear to you." And he marched away, leaving her alone. Pleasant stared at her again, fascinated. He couldn't help it.

She grew pale, turned, and wobbled past his plum castle, out the door.

When evening came, Pleasant was no longer a prisoner of the castle. To keep himself occupied, he had been naming all the beans he had ever heard of: string beans—lima beans—kidney beans—navy beans. But he couldn't wait anymore, and flew over to the cheese section the instant the last blue-and-white apron locked the door. He crawled inside the Swiss cheese, feeling its translucence all around. It gave off a pearly yellow glow; he explored the cool tunnels of it. After he had tried various cheeses, he roamed up and down the shelves.

There were things forbidden to him, since they were sealed tight in glass containers, but whose names he loved pronouncing in the fading light:

BLACKCURRANT JAM

LIME MARMALADE

64

BRAMBLE JELLY

GUAVA JELLY

IRISH GOOSEBERRY JAM

IRISH PLUM PRESERVES

JASMINE PETAL JELLY

He explored fragrant bins, saying their names over slowly—anise drops, eucalyptus drops, glacé mints, maple-sugar blend, butterscotch buttons, filled-raspberry rounds, hazelnut caramels, coffee crunch, triple orange drops, sky-blue mints.

By this time he was growing hungry once more. In the window there were boxes of crackers, standing upright. Skillfully, he broke his way into the boxes, going from Abernathy biscuits to Euphrates biscuits, then over to the wheat bread wafers into the banana chips, then starting from the beginning.

In the midst of this great dinner—the boxes by this time looking like small houses with their front doors invitingly open—he knew he was being watched.

He felt clumsy and fat, but he whirled around as best he could. There were faces pressed against the window on the other side. Faces of people.

What could he do? He did a fast dance for them, flourishing his still-limber tail. The audience encouraged him, so he continued, dancing off his dinner. He became rather pleased with his own ability; and, drawing his inspiration from the color picture on the Euphrates biscuit box, performed a complicated Oriental dance. The audience was beside itself.

However, he could do no more. He was sleepy beyond measure, and curled up right there and fell asleep, dreaming he was a celebrated dancer.

He lived in the store, chewing his way through it craftily, staying by day in the plum castle, dancing marvelous dances at night, in the window, drawing great, enthusiastic crowds. He was very unhappy on

evenings when rain fell, and no audience came.

So, to those who were walking in the City by night, Pleasant acquired a certain fame. However, one morning the plum castle was whisked away. And he was swept into a dustpan and tossed out into the alley behind. Pleasant sat in the shadows of the alley, brooding on how quickly fame vanishes.

And how he wanted desperately to voyage away once more.

Something would happen. Something *always* did.

SIXTH
VOYAGE

THE TEA-STRAINER

The next day was Sunday, and the noisy City was suddenly, utterly, at peace. In the forest, every day continued, the same as the day before—the animals fought and hid and struggled for food and were over-joyed to find themselves among the living. Now, all at once, the City's people were missing. Just like that.

Pleasant did not understand what was happening, how Sunday is different from other days. How could he? Now that he was out of the castle, it made him remember his own house, far away. *Had* he locked the shutters and bolted the door before he had left? He was sure he had, for that was the most pleasant thing to think. He was also trying hard to remember the smell of sweet violets that bloomed in the wild grass outside his door.

The alley was not such a nice-smelling place.

He discovered a book, lying beside the

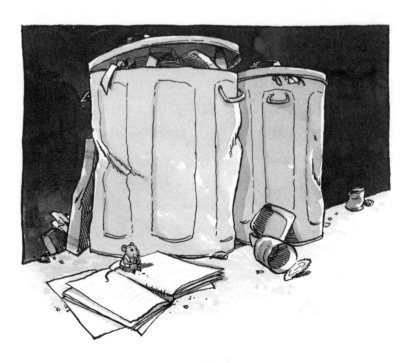

building. He nibbled at the paste and glue of the binding, and finished his meal on crumbs and choice garbage tidbits.

He was suspicious of the lazy hum from automobiles that came roaring, sometimes, up the street at the foot of the alley. But faraway he heard something beautiful, and he couldn't help it, he had to follow it.

He had to follow the throbbing, swelling tune to where it came from; he scuttled along the gutter of the street, protected by the curb. He had to be careful not to plunge into the gaping sewer openings: the wonderful sound did not come from there. He felt the sound rushing down the gutter upon him with the force of a waterfall.

It filled his head, making it ache with happiness.

It was a Sunday organ playing.

When he arrived at the building out of which it flew, he leaped over the curb, leaped over impossible high gray stone stairs, and entered the door, which was open because of the

71

warm weather. The music, however, made him cool.

It was as if he were standing in a field of fresh pink roses.

The organ played *Go Forth, My Heart, and Seek Delight;* then, *All Ye Who Like the Birds Can Soar.*

The high pitch of some of the notes from the organ hurt his ears terrifically, and the low ones, when not only the pipes themselves but the whole floor throbbed, made him feel it deep, to the tip of his tail. But the middle ones soothed him, and he wished he could listen to those forever.

When he reached the organ, he wanted to crawl inside it and live there, even with the high notes and the low ones. He had never heard real music before—except for the music of whistling birds.

There was a lady who loved it also, a lady with beautiful white hair. With her hands she seemed to be (from where he stood) touching the shiny mahogany.

Pleasant touched the organ too with his paws, feeling the music touch *him*. His whiskers trembled.

Then it stopped, like that, except for the echoes of it still stirring in the air, and the lady with beautiful hair was changing her shoes.

Pleasant Fieldmouse waited by her feet. He decided to climb inside one of the empty shoes. He climbed in, just in time, for the shoes were put in a paper bag and the paper bag was put in an automobile and the automobile was, after a jiggling and whirring journey, put in a garage.

The lady was going inside her house (her red-painted house), where perhaps she would sit at an organ. Pleasant tore the smallest of holes in the bag and looked out. Inside the house, the lady with white hair reached in for the shoes. She laid the shoes, one of them carrying him, inside a closet on the floor.

Then she went away. Pleasant lay there comfortably within the shoe, listening.

He wished the shoe had wheels, so he

could move about without getting out. He wondered if someone now had found his raft and was using it? He wondered if he would see the forest again? He wondered if he would always stay with the lady?

At last he crept out of the closet, and explored the quiet bedroom, with all its colors,

and little things—bottles and shells and knick-knacks.

He leaped onto a flowered-print armchair,

and from the armchair he leaped onto the soft big bed with a spread that was the color of grass, where a broad yellow patch of streaming sunlight in the middle made him terribly, terribly sleepy.

Later, the lady with white hair returned to her bedroom. She found him slumbering on her bed, peacefully.

She went out, and quickly brought back her husband.

"Arnold, look. What should we do with him?"

Arnold reflected. "I'll get the tea-strainer." Arnold matter-of-factly went down to the kitchen, where he searched among the drawers and got a tea-strainer with a long, black handle.

He told the lady with beautiful white hair, "This is no place for him; I'm sorry." Carefully he scooped Pleasant up in the black-handled strainer. Pleasant awoke, his tail tingling and one of his ears bent against the wire mesh.

He stirred, and they both knew he was not asleep.

"Oh, Arnold, I can't give him up! What about the birdcage?"

"What do you mean?" asked Arnold.

"You know," she said—"the bamboo one we bought on our last trip to Mexico."

"But you didn't want to keep a *bird* in that; how can you keep HIM?"

"Maybe he'll like it," she replied. "I wish we could keep him."

So she held the tea-strainer and Arnold went to fetch the bamboo birdcage that looked like a cathedral. It had a painted wood clock on the steeple.

They put Pleasant in, together with paper napkins on the floor, and a small tin drinking cup, and a meal of cornbread dipped in gravy. The meal was delicious. Later, the lady brought him some nuts to sharpen his teeth on, though they were not the nuts that were his favorites in the forest.

Pleasant frisked about, inside the bamboo

cathedral, running up and down the bamboo stairs, which were slippery. He especially liked to climb up into the bamboo steeple and stare out into the living room.

In the evenings the lady with white hair, and her husband, Arnold, would sit in the living room—she on the blue sofa, he in the large orange chair—both of them reading. Pleasant wished *he* could be reading. It would give him more to do.

After a while they started lighting fires in the evening in the fireplace with firewood. It was very warm and cozy. They would come and speak to him, and he would run up and down the stairs for them. That was about all there was to do.

In the dark mornings, long before Pleasant himself usually got up, the lady with beautiful white hair and Arnold were down having steaming breakfast coffee.

Then, they would hurry, departing from the house and leaving him alone—and he would spend the day taking naps, so that he could run up and down the bamboo stairs to amuse them in the evening.

Sometimes, the lady would come back in the afternoons to clean the house, or to write letters. There was no organ, there, for her to play. However, she often made music on the phonograph. Pleasant would do one of his dances, just for her, on the cathedral's floor.

For several days, once, rain slapped at the windows. It gave Pleasant a peculiar homesick feeling.

He was sure his own house must be pretty dusty, so he took special pains to keep the birdcage clean, dusting when he had to with his tail, when the lady wasn't looking.

Frost began to brighten the air at night. And the milky moonlight shimmered on the rug.

The lady began to notice that every time she went to the door or her husband walked in, Pleasant stopped whatever he was doing and looked at the open door wistfully. She knew what he was thinking: a birdcage is no place for a fieldmouse.

One Sunday, after she returned, the lady said to Arnold:

"You were right, dear. Please get out the tea-strainer."

She opened the door to the bamboo cathedral, lifting Pleasant gently out, putting him into the strainer.

She tied a silk handkerchief around the basket part of the strainer, so he wouldn't fall out, and spoke to him, telling him not to be afraid. But he *was* afraid, although by now he loved her a great deal.

He trembled when the automobile's engine started, and trembled, from top to toe, while they took him for a long, long ride, which seemed to have no end at all.

The lady with white hair kept speaking to him, and he liked the sound of her whispering, soothing voice. He grew sleepy, lulled by it and the automobile's whirring.

Then the automobile stopped. The silk

handkerchief was removed. Pleasant lay limply, not knowing what he was supposed to do.

"What's that in the back seat?" Arnold was asking.

"A blue balloon," answered the lady with beautiful white hair.

"What's it for?"

"I want to tie it next to where we leave him. I want to know where he is, when we drive away. I can't just leave him—and run off."

"Oh."

So they climbed out of the automobile and walked up a steep hill where dandelions grew in spring. The air was brisk.

And the lady tied the blue balloon to a fallen branch she found, while Arnold set the tea-strainer on its side upon a patch of soft grass, next to it. Pleasant got out.

"Good-bye," said the lady. Then she and Arnold left, looking back over their shoulders to where the bright balloon was bobbing, marking the spot.

They kept looking at the balloon, and she kept
waving at it, as they slowly drove away—
however Pleasant had already run down the
hill on the other side. He was delighted to see
the colors of autumn. He ran under a flock of
oak and maple and mulberry trees.

The leaves started tumbling. Yellow, orange, pink-gold, and red, falling all around

him. The wind would blow, and make them rise again; then they would flutter, flutter, flutter down—with crisp crackling sounds.

Each leaf was bigger than he was. He felt the forest was very near, very near, very near. . . .

ABOUT THE AUTHOR

Jan Wahl was born in Columbus, Ohio and grew up in Napoleon and Toledo. He later studied folk literature and film at the University of Copenhagen where he worked with the late Isak Dinesen and film director Carl Dreyer. Mr. Wahl is the author of numerous beloved children's books including *The Furious Flycycle* and its sequel, the *S.O.S. Bobomobile*. Mr. Wahl's books have won numerous awards including several ALA Notables, the Corretta Scott King Award, the Christopher Medal, and the Young Critics Award at the Bologna International Book Fair. Mr. Wahl regularly lectures and continues to write. He splits his time between Toledo, Ohio and Mexico.